WALT DISNEY'S

Cinderella

W9-APG-909

Adapted by Della Cohen

Illustrated by the Disney Storybook Artists

Long ago in a faraway land, poor Cinderella lived with her mean stepfamily. They filled her days with cooking, scrubbing, washing, and chores of every kind. But Cinderella remained cheerful and kind.

One day, there was a knock at the door. "Open in the name of the King," said the royal messenger. He handed Cinderella an invitation.

Cinderella's stepmother read the invitation. "There's to be a ball in honor of His Highness, the Prince, and by royal command, every eligible maiden is to attend," she said.

Anastasia and Drizella, Cinderella's stepsisters, each imagined she would be the one the Prince would fall in love with.

Surprisingly, Cinderella's stepmother agreed to let her go to the ball, too. "I don't see why you can't go . . . *if* you get all your work done, and *if* you can find something suitable to wear."

While Cinderella raced off to finish her long list of chores, her animal friends got to work. They found an old dress that had belonged to Cinderella's mother. The birds and mice gathered beads and a sash that the stepsisters had thrown away.

Soon they had created a beautiful gown!

Cinderella finally finished her chores and went to her room. But then she realized there was no time to get ready for the ball. She was very sad.

Suddenly, the mice yelled, "Surprise!" They showed Cinderella the beautiful gown.

"Oh, thank you so much!" she cried.

Cinderella put on the gown and hurried downstairs to join the others. But when her jealous stepsisters recognized their old sash and beads, they tore Cinderella's gown to shreds! Then they left for the ball without her.

Sadly, Cinderella went to the garden. All of a sudden, bright, sparkling lights began floating and swirling around her.

Poof! A woman with a magic wand suddenly appeared. It was Cinderella's Fairy Godmother. "Dry those tears," she told Cinderella. "You can't go to the ball looking like that."

"But I'm not going," said Cinderella.

"Of course you are," replied the Fairy Godmother.

The Fairy Godmother waved her magic wand over a pumpkin, and a regal coach appeared!

"Oh, it's beautiful!" said Cinderella.

The Fairy Godmother waved her wand again. The mice turned into four dashing white horses. Then she changed Major the horse into the coach driver, and Bruno the dog into the footman.

Next, the Fairy Godmother turned Cinderella's torn dress into a beautiful gown. In a flash, there were also tiny glass slippers for her feet.

"On the stroke of midnight, the spell will be broken," the Fairy Godmother warned. "Everything will be as before."

The ball was just beginning when Cinderella arrived. The King and Grand Duke watched as the maidens walked forward to meet the Prince. The Prince was unimpressed with them all.

Then he noticed Cinderella.

Entranced, he walked past all the other maidens, and led Cinderella into the ballroom.

They danced every dance together until . . . *bong!* The clock began to strike midnight.

"I must go!" Cinderella cried in a panic.

As she fled, she lost her glass slipper on the staircase.

Bong! The clock sounded its final chime as the coach raced from the palace. It was midnight! The horses turned to mice again. Cinderella was in rags. But she still had one glass slipper.

The next morning, the Prince proclaimed that he would marry the girl who had lost her slipper at the ball. So, the King ordered the Grand Duke to find the maiden whose foot fit the glass slipper.

The news spread quickly. Cinderella was so happy! She hummed to herself as she awaited the Grand Duke's visit.

But her wicked stepmother recognized the tune Cinderella was humming. It was the waltz from the ball! Cinderella was the Prince's love! The stepmother locked Cinderella in her room.

Soon after, Cinderella heard a knock at the front door. The Grand Duke and his footman had arrived!

Meanwhile, Cinderella's mice friends got the key out of the stepmother's pocket and slipped it under Cinderella's door.

Downstairs, the Grand Duke watched as Anastasia tried to squeeze her big foot into the tiny glass slipper. Of course, the slipper did not fit Drizella, either.

As Cinderella hurried down the steps, she called, "Please, wait! May I try on the slipper?"

The angry stepmother tripped the footman as he approached Cinderella. The glass slipper shattered into pieces. "Oh, no!" moaned the Grand Duke.

"But you see," said Cinderella, reaching into her pocket, "I have the other slipper." Quickly, the Grand Duke placed the slipper on Cinderella's foot.

It fit perfectly!

And so, Cinderella married the Prince
and the two of them lived happily ever after.